KT-546-109

MEET ALL THESE FRIENDS IN BUZZ BOOKS:

Thomas the Tank Engine
The Animals of Farthing Wood
Biker Mice From Mars
James Bond Junior
Joshua Jones
Fireman Sam
Rupert
Babar

First published in Great Britain 1993 by Buzz Books,
an imprint of Reed Children's Books
Michelin House, 81 Fulham Road, London SW3 6RB
and Auckland, Melbourne, Singapore and Toronto
Reprinted 1993 (twice)

The Animals of Farthing Wood © copyright 1979 Colin Dann
Storylines © copyright EBU 1992
Text © copyright 1993 William Heinemann Ltd
Illustrations © copyright 1993 William Heinemann Ltd
Based on the novels by Colin Dann and the animation series
produced by Telemagination and La Fabrique for the BBC
and the European Broadcasting Union.
All rights reserved.

ISBN 1 85591 2791

Printed and bound in Italy by Olivotto

The Adventure Begins

Story by Colin Dann
Text by Mary Risk
Illustrations by The County Studio

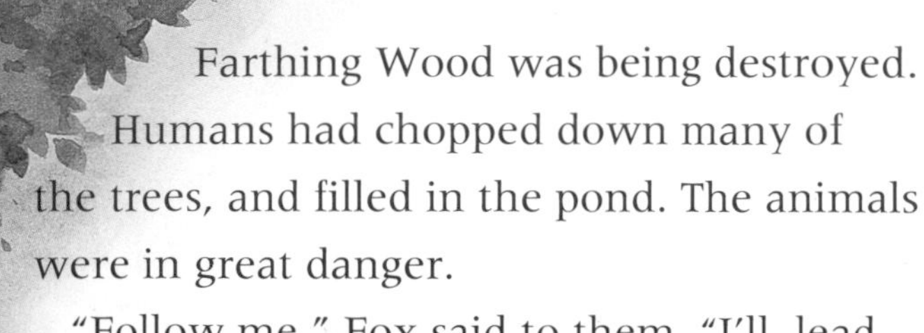

Farthing Wood was being destroyed. Humans had chopped down many of the trees, and filled in the pond. The animals were in great danger.

"Follow me," Fox said to them. "I'll lead you to White Deer Park, a place of safety for us all. It will be a terrible journey, but Toad will show us the way."

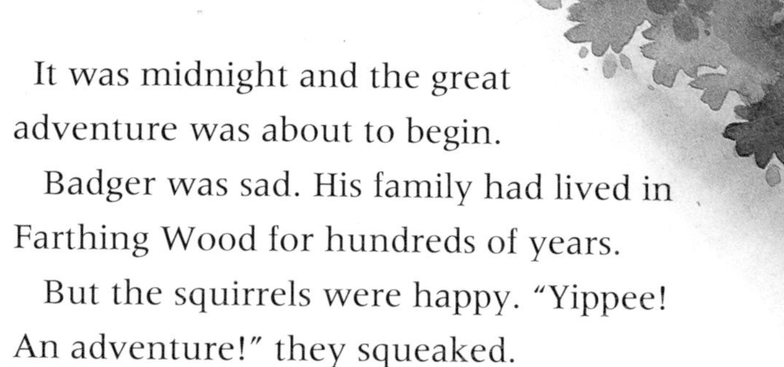

It was midnight and the great adventure was about to begin.

Badger was sad. His family had lived in Farthing Wood for hundreds of years.

But the squirrels were happy. "Yippee! An adventure!" they squeaked.

Poor Mole was worried. "I'm too slow to keep up," he thought.

"Are we all here, Badger?" asked Fox.

Badger looked round at the group of anxious little animals. "Rabbits, hedgehogs, mice, voles, squirrels," he said, counting them off on his claws. "Weasel, Adder, Hare, Owl, Kestrel — "

Quickly Mole hid before Badger could call his name. He was afraid to leave the wood.

"Oh dear," said Badger. "Where's Mole?"

"We've a long way to go before dawn, Badger," said Fox quietly. "We can't wait."

"But we can't leave Mole behind," Badger protested. "I'll stay and look for him. We'll catch you up."

"Right," said Fox. "Now let's go."

The time had come. The little group of animals left their homes in the wood, and set off into the night.

Badger looked round the woodland clearing.

"Mole!" he shouted. "Where's he got to? Silly Moley. Hiding as usual!"

There was no answer. Nothing stirred in Farthing Wood. Then suddenly, a little mound of earth appeared at Badger's feet.

"Mole!" said Badger sternly. "I know you're down there. Come out at once!"

"I'm not coming out," said Mole in a small voice. Badger had to lean over to hear him. "I'm not coming with you. You can beg and plead all you like. I'm staying here."

"But why?" asked Badger.

"Because I'm s-stupid, and s-slow. I can't go as fast as everyone else. I'll hold you up."

"Don't be silly, Mole, old chap," growled Badger. "I'll look after you."

"You will?" gulped Mole.

"Of course," promised Badger.

Mole shot out of the ground. He was smiling now. Gently, Badger picked him up and put him on his back. Then he trotted off after the others.

The animals had been travelling for hours.

"We must find water soon," said the newts, "or our baby will die."

Owl flew off to look for water. Soon she was back.

"Follow me," she hooted. "There's a swimming pool near here. Not far now!"

The little animals struggled over the rough ground, gasping for breath, while Owl led the way. They followed her past a fence and into a garden.

"Water," croaked the newts feebly.

"Quick, over here!" called Owl.

Everyone rushed forward to the pool.

"Don't make a noise," warned Fox. "There are humans about!"

At last the newts reached the pool and dove straight in. They drank and splashed and swam, twisting and turning in the cool water. Their baby was better at once.

Toad bounded in after them. "Come on, mateys!" he called to all the other animals. "Come on in for a swim!"

Everyone crowded round the pool.

"Cor, that's better," slurped Weasel.

"Remarkably enjoyable," spluttered Owl.

"It's not fair! We can't reach the water," the little ones squeaked.

Fox and Badger lay down with their snouts nearly touching the water.

"Run down our backs," said Fox. "You'll be able to drink then."

Toad was having a wonderful time.

“Oo! Whee! Yippee!” he sang happily, as he hopped in and out of the pool. He nearly tipped the rabbits in.

"Don't get us wet!” they squealed.

A light went on in the house.

“Silly Toad!” called Fox. “Now you’ve woken the humans. Get out of the water, everyone! Hurry!”

The animals scrambled clear of the pool.

"Follow Owl," barked Fox. "Badger, help everyone through the fence!"

In the house, more lights went on. Suddenly, the cat flap in the back door swung open, and a cat appeared.

"Grr," he said as the tasty mice filed past.

The cat licked his lips and pushed, trying to force his fat body through the cat flap.

"Fox!" called Badger. "Come quickly!"

Fox hurried to the cat flap, followed closely by Adder.

"What's this?" the cat said when he saw Adder slithering outside his door.

Fox saw his chance while the cat was distracted. Quickly, he slammed the cat flap shut and the cat disappeared.

On and on the animals went. Their tails drooped and their feet dragged in the dust.

Badger heard Mole give a big sigh. "What's the matter, Moley?" he asked.

"I feel bad, riding on you when the others are so tired," said Mole.

Kestrel flew up to Fox. "Kee! Kee!" she called. "Dawn is coming soon, Fox. I'll find a place for us to rest during the day."

Kestrel soon flew back. "There's a big gorse thicket nearby," she told Fox, "but it's on army land, and — " she hesitated.

"Yes?" said Fox.

"We'll have to cross a road to get there," Kestrel answered.

The animals lined up at the edge of the road. Kestrel hovered overhead.

"Go now while there are no cars!" she called. "Quick!"

Badger led the first group. The baby rabbits kept trying to break away.

"Don't panic!" their mother scolded. "Follow Badger!"

"Go! Go!" shouted Fox from the roadside.

Adder led the second group. She looked hungrily at the mice and voles. "Come with me, my dearsss," she hissed.

"Adder, stop teasing," said Fox sternly.

Toad was the last to cross. He hopped into the road. It seemed miles and miles to the other side.

"Come on, Toad! You can do it! Hurry, or you'll get squashed!" his friends shouted.

But Toad was very tired.

"I'm coming, mateys," he croaked feebly. "Toady's coming!"

Suddenly, a huge lorry came roaring down the road towards Toad.

"Oh no!" gasped Toad. "I'm a gonner!"

He rolled over onto his back, and lay still, waiting for the lorry to run him over. To the amazement of the animals, the lorry stopped just in time. The driver got out and bent down to look at Toad.

"What have we got here?" he said.

There was a furious beating of wings in the air. The man looked up as Owl's sharp beak and strong talons scratched at his head.

"Oi! Get off! Stop that!" he said.

"Now's your chance! Run for it, Toad!" the animals shouted.

Toad opened his eyes and sat up.

"I'm not dead!" he said. "Wee hee!"

“I’m coming to get you, Toad,” called Fox.

Owl struck at the man again and he climbed back into his cab, cursing.

Quick as a flash, Fox ran up to Toad. “Catch hold of my tail! Quick!”

Toad grabbed Fox’s tail, and held on tight until they had safely reached the other side of the road.

"You saved my life, matey!" gasped Toad, dropping off Fox's tail.

"And so did Owl," said Fox.

Owl blinked and looked pleased. "It's nice to be appreciated," she said.

It was only a few steps more to the peace and safety of the gorse thicket. Everyone lay down at once.

Gently, Badger set Mole down on the ground. Mole sighed wearily.

"My dear companions," Badger began. "I'd like to say, to one and all, how proud I am to be a member of this valiant company." Badger paused. "Eh? Did somebody say something?"

"Zzzz," snored the other animals.